Daryl Cobb lives in New Jersey with his wife and two children. Daryl's writing began in college as a Theatre Arts major at Virginia Commonwealth University. He found a freshman writing class inspiring and, combined with his love for music and the guitar, he discovered a passion for song-writing. This talent would motivate him for years to come and the rhythm he created with his music also found its way into the bedtime stories he later created for his children. The story "Boy on the Hill," about a boy who turns the clouds into animals, was his first bedtime story/song and was inspired by his son and an infatuation with the shapes of clouds. Through the years his son and daughter have inspired so much of his work, including "Daniel Dinosaur" and "Daddy Did I Ever Say? I Love You, Love You, Every Day."

Daryl spends a lot of his time these days visiting schools promoting literacy with his interactive educational assemblies "Teaching Through Creative Arts." These performance programs teach children about the writing and creative process and allow Daryl to do what he feels is most important -- inspire children to read and write. He also performs at benefits and libraries with his "Music & Storytime" shows.

He is a member of the SCBWI.

Manuela Pentangelo lives in Busnago, Italy, near Milan, with her flowers, family and friends. She was born in Holland, but has lived all of her life in Italy. A student of architectural design, Manuela discovered that her dreams and goals lay elsewhere. She likes to say that she was born with a pencil in her hand, but it took a while before she realized that her path was to illustrate for children. Manuela often visits London, where she likes to sketch at the British Museum, and likes traveling to different places to find inspiration.

She is a member of the SCBWI.

Pirate Words

ahoy - a word used to hail a ship or a person or to attract attention.

crow's nest - a small platform, near the top of a mast, where a lookout has a better view when watching for ships or for land.

sea legs - the ability to balance yourself to the motion of a ship, especially in rough seas.

poop deck - the highest deck at the stern of a large ship, usually above the captain's quarters.

marooned - stuck someplace, usually on a deserted island, with no way off.

yo-ho-ho - no literal meaning, but an exclamation associated with pirates.

matey - a way to address someone in a cheerful fashion.

weigh anchor - to pull the anchor up and leave port.

avast - a command meaning stop.

Blimey! - an exclamation of surprise.

doubloon - a Spanish gold coin.

hands - the crew of a ship.

lad - a way to address a younger male.

lass - a way to address a younger female.

pillage - to steal something by force.

port - a seaport; a location where ships dock.

scallywag - a villainous or mischievous person.

swab - to clean, specifically the deck of a ship.

scurvy - mean and contemptible.

Arr! - an exclamation.

buccaneer - a pirate.

ye - you.

aye - yes.

A+

Pirate Pete

Do Pirates Go To School?

Written by
Daryl K. Cobb

Illustrated by
Manuela Pentagelo

10 To 2 Children's Books

ISBN 978-0-578-05535-0

Written by Daryl K. Cobb
Illustrated by Manuela Pentangelo

10 To 2 Children's Books

Time to Read

TM

Sometimes inspiration can come from the simplest things -- a smell, the sound of a voice, the rustling of trees -- but I never dreamed that a suggestion could spark the creative process. "I wish you had a pirate story. I love pirates," Manuela told me. I thought about it for a moment and said to myself, "I think I just might have one in me somewhere."

Thank you, Manuela, for your idea and for bringing this book to life with your amazing talent and imagination.

Daryl K. Cobb

To: Owen
Keep on reading!

To Daryl, my parents and to all the little pirates that are out there dreaming.

Manuela Pentangelo

Pete was running down the street.
He had some very happy feet.

He found a pair of pirate boots
someone had thrown away.
He couldn't wait to try them on.
It was the perfect day to play.

Pete went right
up to his room
and with no one
else around,

he slipped the boots
onto his feet,

then woke up on
the ground.

"Avast ye mate!"
he heard someone say.

"Why are ye not
in school today?"

"Now, come on boy, it's over there.
Lad, you need some pirate hair."

"It's the biggest ship,
docked in the bay."
That is what he heard Paul say.

On the sign, letters in bold,
read, "Pirate School 200 Years Old."

Sea Dog
Pirate School
200
Years Old

established in 1809
for the higher learn-n of Pirates

Home of the
BT Buccaneers

"Pirates don't just dress this way.
You have so much to learn, I'd say.

Pirate Paul's Class

Pirate Club
Kayley   Riley
Lauren   Conner
Tavi   Sal
Jimmy   Zack
Thomas   Kelly
Holly   Tabitha
William
Elizabeth

First Mates
Braedyn
Clare
Katie
Dominique
Ava
Erin

Pirate Talk 101 is the first class of the day, and 'aye' is the first word that I want to hear you say."

"Aye!"

"'Aye,' means yes. Now everyone, let's say it once again for fun."

"Aye!"

Paul then took out a list
of at least one hundred words.
For an hour straight they studied hard,
and not a single sound was heard.

S.O.S.
Save Our Ship

STRANDED

"Avast," said Paul
"What does it mean?"
Peter took a guess,
"Stop, I think."
"You think?" said Paul,
"Aye," said Peter. "Yes!"

PiRATE PAUL'S
CLASS WAS
HeRe

"Port,"

"pillage"

and "yo-ho-ho"
are all fine pirate words.

"Poopdeck"
prompted quite
a chuckle.

"Avast,"
the students heard.

"You all must learn to swab the deck
and hoist a sail or two.

Listen up, you scallywags,
or we may get marooned.

A crow's nest is not a place
for a bird to fall asleep.

Crow's Nest

A doubloon is the Spanish gold,
in the treasures
that we seek.

"Yo-ho-ho"
doesn't mean a thing,

but it sounds quite nice
when pirates sing.

"Ahoy" is how we say hello
to a fine English lass, and

"blimey"
is the word to use
when you are
late for class.

"Shiver me timbers" is what you say
in a state of complete surprise.
In other words, you say it mate,
when you can't believe your eyes.

Now it's Sword Fighting 101.
Remember, this is just for fun."

The first to try was Pirate Pete.
The crew all cheered and stomped their feet.

Peter moved with style and grace,
he flipped and leaped from place to place.

"Look out!" Paul heard someone say.
A rope had slipped, a mast gave way.

The mast and sail came crashing down,
knocking Peter to the ground.

"Peter, Peter are you okay?"
Peter answered, "Aye, Aye, Aye!"

Avast ye mates, I'm okay."
Then Peter kicked the sheet away.

His mom and dad were standing there,
a little bit confused,
when Peter jumped up from his bed
wearing ladies' shoes.

"Ahoy there, mates!" Peter said
with a yardstick in his hand.
"Pirate Pete is who I am!
You scallywags are on my land.

I hope you brought your sea legs, mates.
Weigh the anchor, set the sail.

We will be casting off right now,
to end this pirate tale."

coloring book

Sea Dog
Pirate School
200
Years Old

established in 1809
for the higher learn'n of Pirates

Home of the
ZZ Buccaneers

Cobb/
Pentangelo 2010

Join the adventure and read!

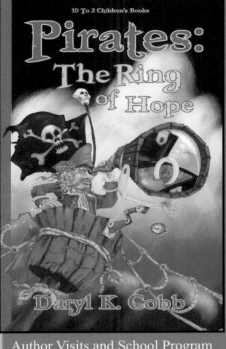

Books & Music
by Daryl Cobb

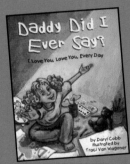

Made in the USA
Columbia, SC
06 October 2017